A Lottie Lipton ADVENTURE

The Scroll of Alexandria

Dan Metcalf

ILLUSTRATED BY
Rachelle Panagarry

darbycreek
MINNEAPOLIS

To Ben & Jake Jolly

Copyright © Bloomsbury Education 2016
Text copyright © Dan Metcalf
Illustrations © Rachelle Panagarry

This Americanization of *The Scroll of Alexandria: A Lottie Lipton Adventure* is published by Darby Creek by arrangement with Bloomsbury Publishing Plc.

Darby Creek
A division of Lerner Publishing Group, Inc.
241 First Avenue North
Minneapolis, MN 55401 USA

For reading levels and more information, look up this title at www.lernerbooks.com.

Main body text set in Stempel Schneidler Std Roman 12/24.
Typeface provided by Adobe Systems.

Library of Congress Cataloging-in-Publication Data

Names: Metcalf, Dan, author. | Panagarry, Rachelle, illustrator.
Title: The scroll of Alexandria : a Lottie Lipton adventure / by Dan Metcalf ; illustrations by Rachelle Panagarry.
Description: Minneapolis : Darby Creek, [2018] | Series: The adventures of Lottie Lipton | Summary: Nine-year-old investigator Lottie and her friends must find the missing scroll of Alexandria to prevent the British Museum's money-hungry Head Curator from selling valuable books to the highest bidder.
Identifiers: LCCN 2016053963 (print) | LCCN 2017006410 (ebook) | ISBN 9781512481815 (lb : alk. paper) | ISBN 9781512481891 (pb : alk. paper) | ISBN 9781512481952 (eb pdf)
Subjects: | CYAC: Museums—Fiction. | Lost and found possessions—Fiction. | Books—Fiction. | British Museum—Fiction. | Mystery and detective stories.
Classification: LCC PZ7.1.M485 Scr 2017 (print) | LCC PZ7.1.M485 (ebook) | DDC [Fic]—dc23

LC record available at https://lccn.loc.gov/2016053963

Manufactured in the United States of America
1-43160-32922-1/30/2017

Contents

Chapter One
London, 1928

"Lottie!"

The cry echoed around the great halls of the British Museum. Lottie turned to look for the source and gulped. She darted into the next hall, past a group of tourists, and into the library, where she bumped into her great uncle, Bert.

"Whoa there! Slow down," he said.

"Sir Trevelyan may have found our science experiment," she blurted out quickly.

"Oh dear," said Uncle Bert, his moustache drooping in worry. "Quick, hide in here. I'll see if I can calm him down."

Lottie quickly hid herself in a nook between some nearby bookcases. The Great Library was one of her favorite places in the British Museum. She had lived in the museum ever since her parents had died in an accident during an archaeological dig in Egypt. Her great uncle, Professor Bertram

West, had sworn to take care of her and had returned to England from Egypt to take a job at the British Museum. They lived in a small, untidy flat on the grounds of the museum, and Lottie loved it. She didn't go to school—instead she was taught by her Uncle Bert and could look at any of the books in the library.

"I don't understand what all these books are doing in a museum," laughed a loud American man to his wife. "Surely they should be in a big library?"

Lottie poked her head out from her nook and smiled.

"Ahem," she coughed politely. "I can

help there." Lottie hopped out of her hiding place. "These books are here by Royal Appointment," she said. "They were left to the museum by King George III after he died. They've been here since 1828, exactly one hundred years."

The couple looked impressed. Other tourists began to gather around.

"Well, aren't you the little bookworm," said the man. "What else can you tell us?" The tourists all looked expectantly at Lottie, who gave them her most welcoming smile.

"The books were collected by King George over his lifetime, but when his son came to the throne, he passed them on to the British

Museum. There are over sixty-five thousand books and maps here, some of which are one of a kind."

Lottie didn't have time to hide again when Sir Trevelyan Taylor, the Head Curator of the Museum, came crashing through the doors. He did not look happy.

"Lottie Lipton!" he bellowed. "How many times do I have to tell you? This is a museum. *Not* your own private playground!"

"Ah, hello, Sir Trev," said Lottie, trying to smile sweetly. The tourists moved into the next room, thanking Lottie as they went. "You found my experiment then?

I was just trying to see what rooms in the museum were best for growing fungus."

Sir Trevelyan looked confused.

"Hmm? No, I meant that you shouldn't leave your toys lying about." He produced Lottie's battered old rag doll, Cleopatra. "This . . . thing was found in the arms of one of the mummies in the Egyptian section."

Lottie grabbed Cleopatra and held her tightly.

"So that's where I left her!" she said. She placed Cleopatra in her cardigan pocket and patted her gently, smiling to herself. Sir Trevelyan humphed and moved over to the bookshelves. He took a tape measure out of his pocket and proceeded to hold it up against the shelves at various angles.

"What are you doing? Ooh, are we getting more books?" inquired Lottie, just as Uncle Bert came huffing and puffing around the corner into the library.

"Sorry, Lottie! He was too fast for me! You'd better—ooh, are we getting more books?" he said, spying the tape measure. Sir Trevelyan didn't even turn around.

"Absolutely not," he scoffed. "We're getting rid of all these useless ones."

Lottie and Uncle Bert's mouths dropped open in shock.

"No! You can't!" cried Lottie. "They belong here!"

Sir Trevelyan turned slowly, his mouth forming an evil sneer.

"I think you're forgetting who runs this museum. I can do whatever I please."

The sound of whistling filled the room, followed by the clank of a mop and bucket. Reg, the kindly old caretaker, poked his head around the corner of a bookcase.

"Hey! What's with the long faces?" he said. "Ooh, are we getting more books?"

Uncle Bert managed to speak up finally.

"Now look here, Sir Trevelyan! These books are here by Royal Appointment. You

can't just pack them away into storage."

Sir Trevelyan laughed to himself.

"Oh, I'm not. I'm going to sell them to the highest bidder."

"That's *outrageous!*" said Lottie, a little louder than she meant to. "They're a collection! They belong together, and they belong *here!*"

Sir Trevelyan finished his measurements and turned to walk out of the room.

"Books, my dear, belong in a library. If you can prove to me that they belong in this museum, then I'll eat my hat," he said with a chuckle. "Reg, close this room. I've got an antique book expert coming just before the museum closes to give me a price for this little lot."

With a slam of the door, Sir Trevelyan was gone. Lottie, Uncle Bert, and Reg all stood in silence, amazed at what they had just heard.

"Uncle Bert, we have to do something," said Lottie, clutching her rag doll for comfort. "We can't let the books leave the museum."

"You're right as always, Miss Lottie," said Reg. "But what can we do?"

The pair turned to look at Uncle Bert, but he was gone. They looked up to find him climbing a ladder to get at the highest bookshelves.

"There's a legend," he called down. "It says that King George collected the rarest books, including the rarest of them all: a scroll from the Library of Alexandria. I've always meant to try and find it, but I never seem to find the time."

"What's so rare about it?" asked Reg.

"The library burned down in the year 30 BC. There are stories, however, that brave men and women ran into the burning building to save some of the scrolls. Only one survived through history. King George found the scroll and then hid it away, as it was too valuable to risk someone stealing or damaging it." Uncle Bert reached for a large, dusty book on the highest shelf and climbed down the ladder. "This book is meant to tell us where it could be hidden."

Lottie was getting excited as she began to see Uncle Bert's plan.

"Ooh, I see! So if we can find the scroll, then Sir Trevelyan would *have* to keep the books. A priceless historical scroll would definitely belong in the Museum and not in a library. So by order of King George, Sir Trev wouldn't be allowed to split up the collection," she said. "Excellent thinking, Uncle Bert! What does the book say?"

"Ah," said Uncle Bert. "That's the tricky bit."

He opened the book and showed Lottie. In small handwriting was a riddle:

> Find the god the Romans called Cupid.
> He flies up high, but don't be stupid!
> Knock three times and you will see,
> Some books are not what they claim to be.
>
> – G.R.

"Written by King George himself!" gasped Lottie. "What does the *R* stand for?"

"*Rex*. It means 'king' in Latin," said Uncle Bert. "You know what this means?"

"Yep," said Lottie. "Another adventure! Come on, you two!"

Can you solve the riddle? Turn the page to see if you're right!

"I don't like riddles. They make my brain hurt," said Reg, scratching his head. Lottie closed her eyes to concentrate.

"Think, Lottie, think," she mumbled to herself. She had heard the name Cupid somewhere before. But where? She paced up and down the row of shelves, trying to remember where she'd seen the name.

"Of course!" she said, making Uncle Bert and Reg jump. "Cupid was the god of love in ancient Rome. I've seen him on Valentine's Day cards."

"Also known as Eros to the Greeks," said Uncle Bert. "He was . . . Lottie, what on Earth are you doing?"

Lottie had grabbed hold of the stepladder and was climbing it to get to the very top shelf in the  library. She reached the top and looked down. She felt dizzy and looked straight back up again.

"It has to be a book," she called down. She scanned the shelves, searching for the most likely title. She had read most of the books there, except the hard-to-reach ones. She reached out and found a large-looking book called *Gods in Ancient Greece*.

Knock three times, the riddle had said, so Lottie rapped on the spine.

Knock!

Nothing.

Knock!

Still nothing.

Knock!

Suddenly there was a *click* from behind the book, and below her a slow *creeeeak* sounded. She whizzed down the ladder excitedly and joined Reg and Uncle Bert, who were staring openmouthed at a large hidden door that had just opened in the center of the bookshelves.

Chapter Two

"Crikey," said Reg.

Lottie was the first to walk toward the open door, followed nervously by Uncle Bert and Reg, who held his mop out like a weapon in front of him. They walked into the gloom of the doorway, and Lottie reached up to the wall to check for a light switch.

"Come on, there must be one somewhere..." she muttered. Suddenly her fingers found the

switch and *pow*! The whole room was lit up.
"Wow!" she cried.

"Goodness gracious," said Uncle Bert.

"A hidden room," said Reg. "You know what this means?"

"What?" asked Lottie.

"A whole new room to clean!" he said, shaking his mop with glee. "More floors to mop, more walls to dust! Oh, joy!"

Lottie shook her head. She could not believe that Reg would actually look forward to cleaning more rooms. Looking around in the gloom she could see the room was small. In the middle of it was a little bookcase. The shelves only held five or six books, which

Uncle Bert was already looking at.

"These are rare . . . very rare indeed. And worth a pretty penny."

"Sir Trevelyan couldn't get rid of them, could he?" said Lottie, crossing her fingers.

"Hmm . . . I'm afraid he might very well try to. It would earn a lot of money," said Uncle Bert. He stood up and looked around at the small dusty room. "I fear that we may have more clues to go before we find the scroll," he sighed and turned back to the books.

"What's so important about this scroll,

then?" asked Reg. He had already pulled a rag from his pocket and had begun polishing the wood-paneled walls around the room, clearing off years of dust and cobwebs. Lottie looked to Uncle Bert to answer Reg's question, but he was too interested in the books he had found.

"The scroll, whatever it contains, is one of the *last* surviving pieces of the Library of Alexandria. It's a hugely important piece of history."

Lottie looked around the room. It was true that the books Uncle Bert was carefully handling were fascinating, but it seemed like they were a distraction to stop treasure hunters

from looking further for the scroll. And they were working! Lottie couldn't let herself get distracted too. *There has to be another clue here somewhere*, she thought to herself.

"Whoever built this room certainly liked ancient Egypt," said Reg, shaking out his dusty rag. "Look at all these hieroglyphics."

Lottie and Uncle Bert turned to look at the walls, which were covered in strange symbols.

"They're not hieroglyphics, old chap," said Uncle Bert. "I don't know what they are."

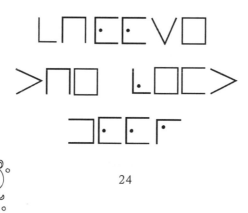

Lottie grinned.

"I do!"

She rummaged in her pocket and pulled out her trusty detective's notebook. She always kept it close by in case she ended up on an adventure. It held all of her best facts and secrets. She flicked through the pages until she found what she was looking for.

"It's pigpen," she said. "A type of code. You use this key to help decipher it."

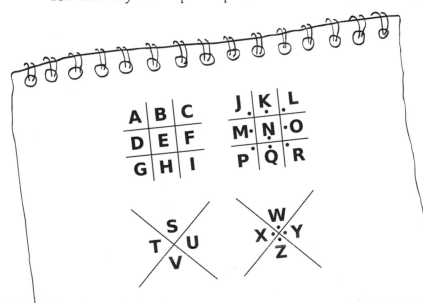

Uncle Bert stared at the notebook for a minute or more.

"Nope," he announced finally. "I haven't got a clue what you're talking about."

Lottie sighed. "The shapes on the wall can be replaced by a letter from the grid. Look, the first shape looks like the third box in the grid, so it's the letter *C*," she said, holding her

notebook up against the shapes on the wall for them all to see. Uncle Bert nodded and whipped out a pencil to start working out the code in Lottie's notebook.

"Here! Look at this," called Reg. He had carried on wiping away the cobwebs from the walls and had discovered two doors set into the wood.

"Looks like our next move," said Lottie. "But which one should we choose?"

Can you decode the message? Which door should Lottie choose? Turn the page to find out if you're right!

The dusty room was awfully silent while Uncle Bert puzzled out the code. "So the first letter is *C*, and the next is *H*," he mumbled to himself. "The next two are the same shape, so they must be the same letter. Hmm, looks like an *O* . . ." Lottie took Cleopatra out of her pocket and nervously held her close. "Aha!" cried Uncle Bert with glee. "Cracked it! Clever stuff, this pigpen code. The message says—"

"Choose the left door," said Reg, interrupting. Lottie and Uncle Bert looked up at Reg, amazed.

"How on Earth did you figure that out so quickly?" said Lottie.

Reg shrugged.

"Just a natural code-breaking genius, I am," he said. Then he broke out in a grin. "Not really. The handle on the left hand door is tarnished, like it has been used lots of times. The other one is shiny—it's never been used."

Lottie and Uncle Bert laughed.

"Clever," said Uncle Bert. With a curious look on his face, he reached for the handle on the right hand door. "I wonder why nobody has ever opened this door . . ."

No sooner had the words left Uncle Bert's mouth than Lottie realized why nobody had ever opened it.

She leaped forward and pulled Uncle Bert back
by the collar of his jacket, just as he opened the
door. He was a big man but luckily didn't have
a great sense of balance. He tipped backward,
landing on his bottom . . .

Pfffft! Pfffft! Pfffft!

. . . just as six sharp darts shot out of the doorway, landing with a *thwang!* in the wooden wall opposite.

"Maybe because it's a booby trap?" said Lottie.

Uncle Bert had gone white with shock.

"Well, King George wouldn't want people to find the scroll easily, now would he?" she reasoned.

"So it seems," said Uncle Bert. "Let's take the left door this time, shall we?"

Chapter Three

Lottie was the first to step forward through the door, and she found herself in a large tunnel. The walls were made of red bricks, which crumbled when she touched them. The ceiling was only a little higher than her head, which meant that she could stand up straight. Poor Reg had to bend over to get in as he followed behind her.

"This tunnel must have been here for hundreds of years," she said. She looked around in wonder. Before Uncle Bert could even duck down to enter the tunnel, she had walked off in the direction of a small speck of light at the end.

"I say, be careful," called Uncle Bert. "You never know what surprises lie around the corner!"

But Lottie was in her own little world, curious and amazed. She often read mystery stories where the detective uncovers a secret passage in an old castle or grand home, but she never imagined that she would find her own secret passage running through her very own museum.

"If I've measured this correctly," began Uncle Bert in a whisper, "then about now we should be passing the main entrance to the museum and the office of—"

"*Ha!* Their faces were a picture," said a voice from nowhere.

Uncle Bert and Reg looked around in confusion for the source of the mysterious voice.

"*Sir Trevelyan!*" hissed Lottie, quietly walking back toward Uncle Bert and Reg. She looked around in a panic but could not see him anywhere.

"The book expert is coming in an hour,"
came Sir Trevelyan's voice again. As Lottie
scanned the walls of the tunnel, she found
where the noise was coming from. She
waved silently at Uncle Bert and Reg and
pointed to the wall next to them. In the
bricks were a few holes, which were just
large enough to look through. Uncle Bert and
Reg pressed their eyes up to the holes, and
Lottie copied them.

"Wow," exclaimed Lottie under her
breath. Peering through the
hole, she could see Sir
Trevelyan's whole office. She
had been there many times,

usually because she had gotten into trouble and had been marched there by one of the security guards. She was looking at the other side of the desk for a change, where Sir Trevelyan sat talking to a friend of his on the telephone.

Somebody wanted to keep an eye on the Head Curator when they built this tunnel, Lottie thought. She saw that Uncle Bert was about to say something, and she quickly pressed her finger to her lips, shushing him.

"Honestly, if we can get rid of those books then we can turn the library into a second office for me. I'd make far better use of it," he laughed. "What's that? Professor West?"

Uncle Bert jumped at the sound of his name. Sir Trevelyan continued.

"Yes, no doubt he and his nuisance of a niece are trying to brew up a way to stop me," he said. Lottie frowned at the insult. "I'd like to see them try. Soon the whole library

will be just up Professor West's alley—
ancient history!"

Lottie turned to see Uncle Bert huffing and
puffing, fuming at the overheard conversation.
She tried to usher them onward.

"Now, now, Professor," whispered Reg
soothingly. "Don't let him get to you. He's just
a big bully, that's all."

"And as for that lazy beanpole of a
caretaker," came Sir Trev's voice through
the wall. "He won't have as much to dust, so

he *should* be happy. Not that
he does any work anyway."

"*What?*" bellowed Reg.

Lottie saw Sir Trevelyan

jump at the sound and look around for the source of the noise. She quickly pushed Uncle Bert and Reg forward into the dark and away from the Head Curator's office.

The tunnel was beginning to get narrower now, and Reg ground to a halt when he got a face full of spiderwebs.

"Ugh!" he said, pulling at the webs. "You go first; I can't see a thing! It's getting a bit bloomin' spooky, if you ask me."

"Oh, my big brave hero," joked Lottie, moving to the front of the tunnel. It *was* very dark now though. "If only we had some sort of light."

Uncle Bert dug around in his pockets and

pulled out a small brass rectangle.

"Will this help?" he said. With a flick of his fingers a flame popped out of the top. "My pipe lighter."

Suddenly they came upon a door. It was old, made of solid oak, and in the center was a handle below two dials surrounded by numbers. Lottie grabbed Uncle Bert's hand and brought the light closer.

"It looks like a combination lock," said Lottie, peering closely at the door. "You turn the dials to the right numbers and pull the handle. If you've guessed the right numbers, the door opens."

"And if you get it wrong?" asked Reg.

"Um . . . another booby
trap?" guessed Lottie. "But
how are we supposed to
work out the numbers?"

While Lottie inspected the
door, Uncle Bert caught sight of a glimmer of
metal on the wall.

"An old gas lamp," he said. "This should
throw some light on the matter."

With a *woosh!* Uncle Bert lit the lamp and
the whole tunnel was illuminated with an
orange glow. He tapped Lottie on the shoulder.

"Shh!" hissed Lottie. "I'm looking for clues."

"I think I may have found some for
you," said Uncle Bert. He pointed to the walls,

now illuminated by the light. They were covered with numbers. Lottie gulped.

$$2 + 5 - 3 + 6 + 5 - 9 + 2 = ?$$

$$7 - 6 + 4 + 9 - 7 + 2 - 4 = ?$$

"That's a lot of math," she said. "We'd better get cracking."

Can you do the math? Take your time and work through them. Continue reading to see if you're right!

The three of them stood in the shimmering gaslight, concentrating on their math.

"Oh, heck," cursed Reg. "I've run out of fingers and thumbs!"

"Shh! Look what you've made me do. I'll have to start again," said Uncle Bert.

Lottie closed her eyes and tried to block out the two grumbling old men.

Let's see, she thought. *Two plus five makes seven. Subtract three to make four. Then add six. That makes ten. Add five to make fifteen, then subtract nine. So I'm left with six. And add two to make . . .*

"Eight!" she announced. "The first number is eight."

"Hmm? Ah yes. That's precisely what I had," said Uncle Bert. He turned the first dial to read eight. "Now, what's next?"

Lottie concentrated again, adding and subtracting, working through each of the steps calmly. She was just about to reveal her answer when—

"Got it!" said Reg. He reached forward and turned the dial to five. Lottie frowned.

"Are you sure?" she said.

"Sure?" said Reg with a grin. He put his hand on the handle and pushed down. "I think I can manage some harmless ma— *waaaaaaaah!*"

Lottie screamed too as a trapdoor opened beneath them, and they all plummeted down into a dark, dark hole.

Chapter Four

Uncle Bert, Reg, and Lottie fell feet first down a steep tunnel. The walls were smooth and formed a kind of slide, which swept them down into the darkness below.

"Waaaaaah!" cried Reg.

"Aaarrrgh!" screamed Uncle Bert.

"Wheeeeeee!" shouted Lottie, who was actually quite enjoying the ride.

They crashed down with a *crunch* onto the

ground, which was cold, gritty, and made of sharp, hard stone. Luckily Lottie fell on top of Uncle Bert, whose large belly acted like a cushion for her. She looked around. Another cold, dark tunnel.

"Oof!" shouted Uncle Bert. "I'm getting too old for this."

"Sorry, Uncle Bert," said Lottie, getting to her feet and giving him a hand up.

"Don't worry, my dear. At least I wasn't crushed by that nincompoop."

Reg turned to face them in the dark, picking up his trusty mop that had

landed nearby. "Who are you calling a nincompoop?"

"You! If you hadn't gotten the number wrong, then we wouldn't be down here."

"There's nothing wrong with my math," said Reg, outraged.

"Be quiet!" said Lottie. She was surprised when the two men actually listened to her. "I think Reg *did* get the number right. The trap door wasn't a booby trap. It was the real door leading to the scroll."

"Then what was behind the door?" said Reg. Lottie shrugged.

"Maybe another booby trap or a distraction?

A fake scroll to put treasure hunters off the scent of the real one?" she guessed. "Uncle Bert, I can't see a thing down here, can you light your pipe lighter again?"

Uncle Bert started to search his pockets for his lighter.

"If the trap door was the correct door, then the scroll or the next clue must be down here somewhere," said Reg.

Lottie nodded. Suddenly a light appeared behind her.

"Ah, that's better. Thank you, Uncle Bert."

She could see her surroundings more clearly now. It was a large tunnel, completely circular and built with bricks. On the ground

were two long, gray metal
rails that seemed to go
on forever.

"Um . . . Lottie, my dear,"
said Uncle Bert with a note
of worry in his voice. "I don't have my pipe
lighter. I must have dropped it."

Lottie gulped. The tunnel rumbled.

"Then where is that light coming from?"
she asked, not sure if she wanted to know
the answer. Reg turned around and raised his
finger. He began to shake and stammer as
he pointed ahead of him. At the end of the
tunnel, two bright lights approached, getting
closer and closer and closer.

"T-t-t-*train!*"

The rumble increased to a roar, then to a clatter, and then to a deafening din as Lottie realized that they were standing in a subway tunnel used by the London Underground.

"Run!" she yelled. Uncle Bert and Reg followed. The train honked. Lottie sprinted, panicking that the twenty-seven tons of steel behind them was never going to stop.

The lights of the train flashed across the tunnel, and Lottie searched for a way out. Suddenly the lights bounced off a wall ahead and showed an alcove, a small space in the wall for workmen to stand in an

emergency. She wasn't sure if the three of them would fit, but it was their only chance.

"This way!" she called over the noise of the train and grabbed the two men by their sleeves. She could feel the hot air of the train engines on her neck as she dived into the alcove, just in time.

With a *bang!* and a *clang!* the train rattled past them, a few confused faces inside the carriages looking back at them. The train rattled away and Lottie looked over at Uncle Bert and Reg.

"Still think that wasn't a booby trap?" said Uncle Bert. They squeezed back out of the alcove into the tunnel.

"I . . . I don't understand," said Lottie. "We got the math right. Why would it lead us to the London Underground?"

Reg and Uncle Bert leaned against the wall of the tunnel, out of breath from all the exercise. Uncle Bert scratched his balding head.

"Of course, the books came to the museum one hundred years ago," he said, thinking out loud. "When the Underground wasn't even built. Perhaps the scroll was buried in a secret chamber and the tunnel came along *after* that?"

Lottie perked up, smiling from ear to ear.

"So it wasn't a trap? The slide led us to the scroll! We just have to find it."

She dashed back along the tunnel to where they had been spat out by the slide. Reg and Uncle Bert followed, huffing and puffing their way along the tracks.

"Hang on," called Reg, out of breath. "How do we know the scroll is still here?"

He had a point. Lottie looked around in the gloom, the only light now coming from the gaslight in the tunnel above them.

She searched around for anything to point them toward the scroll. "Aha!" she said, spying a sign on the side of the tunnel. "Because they left a clue!" Lottie whipped a handkerchief from Uncle Bert's breast pocket and rubbed the soot and dust from it. Slowly, she revealed a message:

HTE LOCRLS SIEL WEBOL UROY TEEF.

"Gibberish," said Reg. "Always gibberish."

"Anagrams," corrected Lottie.

"Anna who? Never heard of her," said Uncle Bert. Lottie sighed. For a professor of Egyptology, her great uncle could be quite dim sometimes.

"Anagrams. They're words that have their letters scrambled up. We just have to unscramble them."

Reg peered at his pocket watch.

"Then we'd better crack on. That book man will be here soon."

Lottie concentrated on the sign and tried to get her brain to unscramble the letters, but she was nervous and panicking.

Can you help Lottie? Unscramble the letters to find the scroll. Continue reading to see if you're right!

Lottie could hear the tick-tick-ticking of Reg's pocket watch as she desperately tried to work out what the sign said.

Okay, the first word is . . . Eth? No—"The"! *Ooh, that was easy,* thought Lottie. Slowly it came to her:

"The . . . scroll . . . lies . . . below . . . your . . . teef. I mean, feet!" she said. They looked down at the bare earth below the sign and Lottie sighed. "How are we supposed to dig that up?"

Reg stepped forward with an unusually serious look on his face.

"Step aside, Miss Lottie." He held out his mop for her to hold.

Lottie did as she was told and watched as old Reg bent down and used his hands like shovels to dig up the mud. Scoop after scoop, he chucked handfuls of mud behind him at an amazing speed. It was like watching a dog retrieve a long-lost buried bone. Within minutes he had hit something in the dirt.

"Jackpot!" he yelled. He lifted out a small stone box. It was long, thin, and covered in Egyptian hieroglyphs. Lottie and Uncle Bert were still staring at his muddy hands in amazement. "I was a trench digger in the Great War," he explained. "Shovels just slowed me down."

"Brilliant, Reg. That was remarkable," said
Lottie. "But we don't have time to look inside.
Let's get up to the museum, and fast!"

Chapter Five

Sir Trevelyan Taylor paced the floor of the library, his footsteps echoing in the empty room. He pulled out his gold pocket watch just as the ornate clock at the end of the room struck six o'clock.

"Where is he?" he muttered to himself. He plunged his hands into his pockets and started to pace once more.

"Sir Trevelyan, I assume?" said an old man

in a tweed jacket and gold-rimmed spectacles. The two men shook hands. "I'm Reuben Ford, expert in antiquarian artifacts." Sir  Trevelyan looked confused. "That's old books to you."

"Ah! Good. We certainly have a lot of those," said Sir Trevelyan. "Now, how much—"

"*Stop!*"

The two men jumped with fright and turned to look at the door, which burst open with a bang. Lottie, Uncle Bert, and Reg walked in, out of breath and covered in mud, dust, and grime.

"*Stop in the name of the King!*" shouted Lottie.
"Well, kind of . . ."

"What on Earth? Professor West, control your child!" said Sir Trevelyan. "Ugh! You're filthy! And what's that smell?"

Uncle Bert blushed.

"Ah, sorry about that. We had to come through a sewer to get back to the surface."

Reg waddled closer and placed the heavy
stone box on a table with a grunt.

"Hmm," said Reuben Ford, inspecting it
closely. "This looks interesting."

He carefully ran his fingers over the
markings on the box. "Egyptian? May I?"

Lottie nodded and they all gathered
around as he lifted the lid.

Inside was a scroll made of thin papyrus, wound around wooden poles. It lay on a bed of velvet, and tucked underneath was a letter on much more modern notepaper. Lottie picked it up and read it aloud.

To whom it may concern,

You see before you the last remaining scroll from the Library of Alexandria. It is part of my book collection but had to stay separate because of its value. If found, it should be returned to the collection and never separated from it. The books and scroll must always stay together.

By order of the Crown,
George R.

"This must be priceless. Over two thousand years old," said Sir Trevelyan, his eyes lighting up at the thought of more money. He turned to the book expert. "How much?"

Reuben Ford placed the lid carefully back on the box.

"As you say, it's priceless, so I cannot offer anything for it."

"What?" exploded Sir Trevelyan. Lottie grinned.

"The scroll belongs here, with the rest of King George's books," she said.

"And you can't sell any books from the library. They have to all stay together," said Uncle Bert.

"Says who?" Sir Trevelyan was red-faced now, boiling with anger.

"The King," said Reg proudly. "And you can't argue with *him*!" He thrust the royal note at the Head Curator. Sir Trevelyan looked from the note to Reuben Ford, who nodded in agreement.

"Oh dear," said Uncle Bert. "You seem to have turned a distressing shade of red, Sir Trevelyan! Perhaps you should sit down with a nice cup of tea?"

"And a large helping of your own hat?" said Lottie with a smirk.

"Agh! I'll get you for this, Professor West!" shouted Sir Trevelyan. He turned to Lottie, who quickly hid her smirk. "And you, you little pip-squeak!"

He stormed away like a bad loser, slamming the door behind him as he went.

Several days later, Lottie found herself in all the newspapers. She saved all the clippings and pasted them into her scrapbook, alongside her amateur archaeologist certificates and autographs of famous detectives she had met.

Uncle Bert had wasted no time, and the Scroll of Alexandria was already in a glass cabinet in the library, ready to be unveiled to the public. The photographers were ready and waiting, and Lottie had even put on a posh dress for the occasion.

"Ready, my dear?" said Uncle Bert. He offered her his hand, and they walked through the museum together, pausing only for Lottie to re-tie Uncle Bert's bow tie. They came to the library and walked in to the sound of applause. Photographers went up to the glass case, which was covered with a sheet and guarded by Reg.

"Lottie, this was your find. Be my guest," said Uncle Bert, helping her up onto a box to speak to the crowd.

"This way, Miss Lipton!"

"*Give us a smile!*" shouted the photographers.

Lottie cleared her throat.

"Ladies and gentlemen, it gives me great pleasure to present to you the ancient Scroll of Alexandria!"

She pulled the sheet off with a flourish, and the crowd gasped and applauded. Then suddenly, from deep within the museum, she heard a cry.

"*Argh! Lottie!*"

She looked around and gulped.

"What on Earth was that?" said Uncle Bert. Lottie turned to him with a worried look.

"I think Sir Trevelyan has *definitely* found our fungus experiment this time!"

Glossary

anagram: a word made by rearranging the letters of another word

antiquarian: someone who deals in old books or antiques

Cleopatra: Queen of Egypt who reigned from 51 BC to 30 BCE

Cupid/Eros: the winged god of love. The Greeks called him Eros, and later the Romans called him Cupid.

curator: person in charge of a museum

gibberish: nonsense

King George III: King of Great Britain from 1738–1820

Library of Alexandria: a large library in Alexandria in ancient Egypt. It burned down in the Third Century AD.

London Underground: a network of underground trains in London, which opened in 1863

papyrus: a thin material made in ancient Egypt for writing or painting on

scroll: a roll of parchment, paper, or papyrus

Brain Teaser

See if you can crack these anagrams!

Rearrange the letters to make words and characters found in this story:

ERG _____

EMUMUS _____

DERAILANAX _____

PEIP ELGIRTH _____

NODNOL UDDERRUNGON _____

ALERTENVY RAYLOT _____

TOELIT NITPOL _____

NUCLE TEBR _____

Did You Know?

- The pigpen cipher was first used in the 1700s by a secret group of people called the Freemasons.

- The British Museum used to have its very own Underground station. It closed in 1933 but is still down below the ground!

- The Library of Alexandria was destroyed in the Third Century, but was rebuilt on its original site in Egypt in 2002.

Crack the Code

Use the key on page 16 to work out the message below. Good luck!